BLITZ

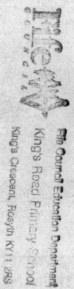

BLITZ

ROBERT WESTALL

ILLUSTRATED BY
DAVID FRANKLAND

Collins
An *Imprint of* HarperCollins*Publishers*

First published in Great Britain
by Collins Audio in 1994
First published by Lions in 1995
and reprinted in Collins

14 16 18 19 17 11 15

Collins is an imprint of
HarperCollins*Publishers* Ltd,
77-85 Fulham Palace Road,
Hammersmith, London W6 8JB.

Printed and bound in Great Britain by
Omnia Books Limited, Glasgow

CONTENTS

NOTE FROM THE AUTHOR

A brief word about the stories. All the startling facts –
the Bren gun carrier in the school, the 'ruined city of
Kor' itself, the deadly euphoria of the pilot after the
crash, the crazy events of the night of Operation
Cromwell – are all either from my own experience or
well-documented in studies of the time. However, the
haunted shelter in Liverpool is, I think, no more than
urban legend, though the pigswill dumps and drunks
were all too real. Liverpool did have large brick surface
shelters because lack of gardens in the poorer suburbs
made Anderson shelters impossible.

THE
RUINED
CITY OF KOR

As soon as the bombing of Tyneside got bad, the timber-yards down by the river moved their wood piles out into the open fields.

Albert Bowdon and I were the first to find them, on Lawson's Farm. We were cycling around as always, looking for war souvenirs and trouble.

Lawson's was a favourite calling-stop, right out beyond the edge of town. It had been sold to a house builder just before war broke out, but the farm-buildings still stood, a marvellous place for the gangs to practise street-fighting each other, shinning up the ladders into the haylofts. Though no matter how hard you machine-gunned the enemy with your wooden tommy-gun, no matter how hard you shouted *"Wa-wa-wa-wa!"* he would never admit to being dead. Just say you'd narrowly missed and go on fighting.

There was also, at Lawson's, the head-high walls of a street of new houses, frozen dead by the War. We called it the Maginot Line 'til the French surrendered to the Nazis, after which we slowly kicked it to bits, brick by brick, in disgust.

Lawson's was deserted that night because it was a long walk from town, and the gangs usually saved it for weekends. But, looking through Lawson's wildly overgrown hedge, we saw a new city grown up like mushrooms overnight. A city of many streets, and pale gold and white buildings. A city of flat roofs, which gave it an eastern look, like something in the background of a Christmas crib; which was why we called it the Ruined City of Kor.

It was the smell that told us it was a city of solidly-piled wood. The sweet smell of pine and resin and mahogany. Kor never again smelled as sweet as it did that night. We climbed through the streets between, giving them names because we were the first. The Street Called Straight, the main thoroughfare was named that night; and the Street of the Goldsmiths.

And the uneven lengths and piling of the wood made little caves where you could hide and plot, or keep dry in the rain, or even, greatly daring, light camp-fires.

Later, there was a sidestreet of caves used by lads who'd got taken short or couldn't be bothered to walk home, and that got called Rotten Row. People brought chalk and paint, and labelled the streets with their names in big scrawling letters.

Of course it was a nuisance when men came with lorries during the day, when we were at school, and took our buildings away, or built new ones. But they were never there when we were, not even a night-watchman; even the old gaffers had gone for war work.

There were two games we played in the Ruined City of Kor, besides street-fighting. If several gangs got together, you had 'Breakout from Stalag Luft VI' which was a marvellous chase over the piles and the long planks we laid between them, miles above the ground.

But even if there were only two of you, you could still play 'Paratroops'. From the tallest pile, a plank sloped down at forty-five degrees, a plank smoothed over the weeks by a hundred bums – and one or two tin trays, when the plank was new and full of splinters. But what did a few splinters in your bum matter? Britain stood alone; it was a time for courage. You whizzed down the plank at breathtaking speed, pushed up your kid's tin hat when it fell over your eyes, and machine-gunned everything in sight in a mad rage.

Albert and I were playing 'Paratroops' the evening things really happened. Our mothers hadn't wanted to let us come because there'd been a lot of daylight raids that week, and they were nervous. But it was a lovely golden evening, with the barrage balloons up so high that the setting sun winking on their silver sides made them look almost like stars.

People thought then that if the barrage balloons were high, there wouldn't be a raid. They used them like the weather forecast.

How wrong they were! I was just picking a splinter out of my bum when the siren went.

No, we weren't terrified. We just got that little sinking feeling in our guts. We were old hands at air-raids. Nobody ever panicked; everybody else would have sneered at them – their lives would've been misery for months afterwards.

I just looked at Albert and he looked at me. We were over two miles from home and the siren only gave you a couple of minutes warning before the bombers were on you.

"Dig in?" I said. And Albert nodded.

We went and dragged our bikes into the deepest cave and squatted over them. We didn't feel in any danger from falling shrapnel, not under twenty feet of wood. Not unless Jerry dropped incendiary bombs on us, and then we could still get out fast, before the whole place went up in flames.

"It'll only get you if it's got your number on it," said Albert.

"Me mam'll be worried," I said.

"No point," said Albert. "If we try and belt home, some warden will only shove us down the nearest shelter."

"We gotta good view."

Normally, in raids, I was down our shelter, with nothing to stare at but a pile of sandbags our dog had peed on more often that I care to remember. But now I could see the whole town spread out before me. The gasworks, the masts and funnels of the ships in the river.

"There they go," yelled Albert. And I caught a fleeting glimpse of a handful of long thin shapes streaking over the works chimneys down by the river. "Keeping low so the guns can't get them."

"If the guns don't get them the fighters will…"

"Hurricanes from Usworth and Spitfires from Acklington," we chorused together, with great satisfaction. "Gonna be a dogfight."

And then we began to hear the machine-guns up in the clouds; they sounded like a boy running a stick along a row of iron railings. Only lots of boys, and lots of railings.

"Goin' out for a look," said Albert.

But he never did. Because at that moment we heard the engines. Howling, screaming. Coming straight at us like the end of the world. Louder and louder and louder 'til it couldn't possibly get any louder. Only it did.

The noise pressed you flat like a huge hand. And kept on pressing. Just when I had given up all hope, and Albert's mouth kept opening and shutting and no sound came out, a great fat Jerry plane, a Heinkel, whizzed into view, all pale-blue belly and the machine-gun underneath sparking away like a firework.

And then it was just a dwindling speck, and the stink from its smoking exhausts.

"There was a British fighter after that Jerry," said Albert. "The Jerry was shooting at it."

"Where is it then?" I said.

It was then we heard the crash. It was like the night me mam pulled the Welsh dresser over, trying to hang up the Christmas decorations, only worse.

Then silence. Only a dog barking in the distance.

"Something's got shot down," said Albert.

"Wasn't the Jerry."

"Oh God."

We sort of screwed up, like when the opposing team score the winning goal. It was an awful feeling.

"Shall we go and look?"

"He might be trapped... He might be..."

It was unsayable. But we went.

It took a long time to search ruined Kor. Expecting at every corner...

But what we found was a surprisingly long way off. A new row of furrows in the field beyond Kor, as if a farmer with six ploughs joined together had...

And a gap in the hedge that something had vanished through. Something definitely British, because a lump of the tail had fallen off, and lay with red, white and blue on it.

We tiptoed through the gap.

It looked as big as a house.

"Spitfire."

"Hurricane, you idiot. Can't you tell a Spitfire from a Hurricane yet?"

"It's not badly damaged. Just a bit bent."

I shook my head. "It'll never fly again. It looks... broke."

The tail was up in the air; the engine dug right into the ground, and the propeller bent into horseshoe shapes.

"Where's the pilot?"

"He might have baled out," suggested Albert, hopefully.

"What? At that height? His parachute would never have opened. Reckon he's trapped inside. We'd better have a look."

"Keep well back," said Albert. "There's a terrible smell of petrol. I saw petrol take fire once..."

There was no point in mocking him. I was so scared my own legs wouldn't stop

shaking. But it was me that went a yard in front.

The cockpit canopy was closed. Inside, from a distance, there was no sign of any pilot.

"Baled out. Told ya," said Albert.

"With the canopy closed?"

"The crash could've closed it, stupid."

"I'm going to have a look."

I don't think I would have done if I'd thought there was anybody inside. I edged up on the wing, frightened that my steel toe and heel caps would strike a spark from something. The smell of petrol was asphyxiating.

He was inside.

Bent up double, with only the back of his helmet showing. And there was a great tear in the side of the helmet, with leather and stuffing... and blood showing through.

"He's a dead 'un," said Albert, six inches behind my ear. I hadn't even heard him come – he was wearing gym-shoes. "Look at that blood."

I felt sick. The only dead thing I'd ever seen was the maggot-laden corpse of a cat in the ruins of Billing's Mill.

"Let's go an' fetch the police," said

Albert. "They deal with dead 'uns."

I was just edging carefully back down the wing, when a flicker of movement in the corner of my eye made me jump.

The dead 'un was sitting up.

The dead 'un was looking at me with two bright blue eyes.

The dead 'un grinned at me. Made a little 'hello' gesture with his gloved hand. My terror turned to rage. I was so angry with him because he wasn't dead. So I hammered on the closed canopy and shouted, "Open up, open up!" like a policeman.

His hand went up, and he undid a catch and pushed the canopy back, where it locked open.

"Hi, kids." He sounded American, or at least Canadian.

"Boy, have I got a headache! Haven't got a fag, have you?"

I didn't think. I had a fag and a half, in an old tobacco tin, that I'd pinched from my father's cigarette case. We sometimes came to Ruined Kor to smoke, in secret. And now I got it out. I mean, the RAF were our heroes, the Brylcreem Boys...

Albert gave one look at my box of matches and fled. Screaming about petrol.

It was then that I realised the dean 'un mightn't be dead, but he was in a pretty queer way. That bullet in the head must have driven him mad; his brain was not working right...

"Come on," I shouted. "Get out. You can't stay here."

He just grinned lazily again. "What's the hurry, kid? It's a lovely evening. Let's take it easy."

I looked at where the engine was. The engine-covers had crumpled up and I could see the engine. And feel it. It was so hot it was practically giving my bare knees a sunburn.

As I watched, some liquid dripped on to it and vaporised into a puff of white smoke. Then a little shower of electrical sparks...

I ran like hell. I didn't stop running for fifty yards, I was so terrified the plane was going to blow up.

We stood and watched him from a safe distance. We saw the heat-shimmer rising from the engine, the petrol oozing dark from the tank in the fuselage behind his head.

And he went on smiling at us, waving to us.

"Like he's on his holidays," whispered Albert.

I just wanted to run away. The idea of seeing him smiling one minute, then frizzling up like a moth in a candle-flame the next...

Then I had my brainwave. I took out my tobacco tin and waved the whole cigarette at him. Greatly daring, edging towards him, at a distance of thirty yards, I lit up the half-fag and blew a luxurious smoke-ring in the still evening air.

It worked. He bellowed, "For God's sake, kids," and began to heave himself out of the cockpit with a big grimace.

The first time it didn't work. The second time he managed to remember to undo his parachute and safety-harness.

Then he was weaving slowly across the grass towards us, like the town drunk. Snatched the fag off me, cupped his hands round mine, which were shaking so much I could hardly strike a match, took a big drag, and fell flat on his back, and lay there laughing up at us and blowing much better smoke rings than mine, and groaning what a headache he had.

"We're still too close," screamed Albert,

looking at the plane. "Get up, Mister."

The pilot just lay there and laughed.

"Grab his feet," said Albert. We dragged him away by main force, 'til his boots came off in our hands. But fortunately there was no blood inside, just some rather smelly socks and...

"He's wearing silk stockings," said Albert, incredulously. "Women's silk stockings."

"Lot of them do," I said. "Keeps them warm. Keep pulling."

So we dragged him, still laughing and shouting, "Lay off, kids." And so we got him to a safe distance, and put his boots back on, him giggling and saying that we tickled.

"'Nother fag, kid?" he said.

I said, with low cunning, "Haven't got any more. But me dad's got plenty. I'll take you to him, if you'll get up and walk."

We got him up and walking in the end. But to keep him pointing in the right direction... He would wander off to one side to admire a dandelion. Or a pile of dog-dirt.

"S'funny. Dog-dirt's a beautiful brown. But nobody likes it."

When we reached the first houses there wasn't a soul in sight. It was then I realised the air-raid was still on. Down in the town, two bombs exploded. The guns were firing at something above the clouds, and shrapnel from the exploding shells began to rain down. We tried to drag him towards a shelter, but he just went blundering on like a great bull out of control. And we hadn't the heart to leave him...

In the end, we were picked up by a policeman.

Who said, sharply, as if we were little criminals, "What are you boys doing with that airman? Give him to me. And get down a shelter immediately."

He didn't wait to see us do it, but we knew we'd be in trouble if we followed him.

We turned, and looked back at Lawson's Farm.

We might have lost our pilot, but we still had our plane...

*

It took fire when we were halfway back. All we could do was watch it burn. It must have been one of the earliest Hurricanes, with wooden wings as well as a wood-and-fabric body. It burnt fast; within half an hour there was just the engine and the tyreless wheels, and the machine-guns and a blackened tangle of wires, and a lot of white ash, the shape the wings had been.

All too hot to grab as souvenirs.

Then the all-clear went, and in five minutes my dad was there on his bike.

"Thought I'd find you here," he said. "Where were you in the air-raid?"

He was as mad as hell with me, for worrying him and me mam so much, so I just said, "A woman had us down her shelter."

If I'd told him the truth, I think he would have taken off his belt and larruped me there and then. Terrible man, my dad.

"C'mon home to bed," he said, very fiercely. "This minute."

"Can't we stay 'til it cools? For souvenirs?"

"I won't speak to you again," he said. "Where have you left your bike? I hope nobody's pinched it..."

What more could I do? What more can I say? There was a whole crowd of kids gathering by that time, avid for souvenirs.

When we went back the following day, thieving kids had stripped the site bare. There wasn't a scrap, except the big engine and bent propeller. And the RAF soon sent a lorry to take that away.

I think every kid in the district was carrying round a bit of that Hurricane, except us.

But we still think it was our Hurricane. And we shall carry our secret to the grave.

THE
THING
UPSTAIRS

Maggie came slowly out of school and instinctively looked up at the sky. But there were no German bombers; just one high thin vapour-trail which was the Germans photographing England, getting ready for their invasion. Photographing every house, Billie Cramer said, every garden. So the Gestapo would know where to come to arrest you. But Billie Cramer was such a liar...

Below the school on its cliff, the Channel lay blue and peaceful. But from the far side, from the dim shadow of the French coast, there was that low rumble that never ceased. The German guns around Dunkirk. Hemming the British in. Hemming their dads in.

Some dads had escaped and were home on leave. Tony Milburn's dad was, limping with the aid of two sticks. But still in khaki uniform, still with his rifle in the cupboard at home in case the Germans came. Aggie

Phipps' dad fetched her from school every night, in his filthy oil-stained battledress. As if he was afraid the Germans might steal her; he hugged her so tight.

But of Maggie's dad there was no sign. He was still over there, somewhere, with his beloved lorry that he called 'Martha'.

The boys had been playing a game called 'Dunkirk' for days. Tearing round the yard machine-gunning everyone on sight, even the Head, with invisible machine-guns, going *"Wa-wa-wa!"* with their mouths.

Pretending to throw hand-grenades and waiting for the explosion with their hands over their ears and eyes as wide as saucers. Falling dead with widely flung arms and excruciating screams, only to leap up again immediately to machine-gun somebody else.

Boys were stupid. Dunkirk wasn't a game; Dunkirk was where your dad was.

But ever since this morning, the boys had given up playing 'Dunkirk'. Instead, at every possible opportunity, they gathered in the corner of the yard and stared into the bike-shed.

For inside the bike-shed, when they arrived for school that morning, they had discovered a little tank. At least the boys said disparagingly, it wasn't a *real* tank. It was called a Bren carrier and it had no turret, just a tarpaulin fastened securely over its open top. And it was no bigger than a car.

At first they just stood and stared; standing in a circle four boys deep, so no girl could get near, even if a girl wanted to. They admired its great muddy cogs, and the caterpillar tracks, and the strange painted symbols on its side, and argued about what they meant.

And then they began to wonder what lay inside, under the tightly-stretched tarpaulin. A Bren gun, or even dead soldiers...

Billie Cramer began to untie the ropes that held the tarpaulin in place, while the rest waited agog, their hearts thumping painfully in their heaving chests. Billie took a long time; he made the most of it, being a show-off. Saying he recognised the smell of a dead body.

But when he finally threw back one corner of the tarpaulin, with a fairground flourish, all there was was a half-eaten tin of bully-beef that ponged to high heaven, a pair of boots that ponged even worse, and a copy of an old French newspaper called

Figaro that had been torn into quarters for use on the lav.

And then the Head had arrived like an avalanche, grabbed Billie painfully by the ear and hauled him into school for a caning. Since then, Old Brimbly the caretaker had stood on guard over it, grim as a policeman in his old brown overall. The boys dared do nothing, but they still stood staring at the huge muddy object, as if the solving of all Britain's problems lay within.

And all day long through lessons, they had heard the Head screeching down the telephone in his study, for someone to take the hideous great thing away. But it seemed that no one would, for he was still yelling down the phone, his voice hoarse, when Maggie passed his door on the way out of school.

She didn't linger. She had much worse things to worry about than hoarse headmasters or Bren gun carriers. Worse things even than Dad being still in Dunkirk.

She was terrified her mum was going mad.

Mum had been all right till two days ago. Tight-lipped, pale, worried to death like everyone else's mum, but normal.

And then yesterday morning she'd come to Maggie's room to wake her up and the pinched, worried look was gone. She looked ten years younger, rosy-faced like a young girl.

She had sat on the bed and said, "It's all right, Maggie. Everything's going to be all right after all." And she had hugged Maggie so tight that Maggie had felt she was being squeezed to death.

And Mum had laughed strangely, deeply. And then Mum had wept a little, because Maggie could feel Mum's tears sliding down to her scalp through her hair. Mum, laughing and crying at the same time...

"*What's* all right, Mum?"

"Oh... everything," said Mum, deliberately uncertain and vague. "*Everything* is going to be all right."

"Is Daddy home?"

She felt her mother give a start, then she said, "Heavens, no. No sign of Daddy. I expect the Army still needs him and his lorry round Dunkirk. The men are still being brought home, you know. I expect Daddy's making himself useful."

How could everything be all right, when Daddy was over there, being shelled by the Germans? When he might be killed at any minute?

But before she could ask any more questions, Mum was heading for the door. Humming to herself, 'til she caught herself at it, and stopped.

And all through breakfast, Maggie kept catching Mum with that idiotic blissful look on her face...

But that night, when she got home from school, the silly-happy look was gone. Mum's face was pale again, worse than before, and pinched up. And Mum started at the least sound, even at perfectly normal sounds like the gas stove clicking as it cooled down after cooking the supper; or the alarm clock going off by accident upstairs.

And when old Mrs Greenough had knocked on the front door, wanting to borrow half a cup of sugar, Mum had gone paralysed and just sat there, while knock after knock came on the front door, and finally Maggie had had to go to answer it.

"It's only Mrs Greenough, Mum, wanting her usual..."

Mum just sat there, clutching her throat with one hand, and the area over her heart with the other.

Finally she swallowed three times and said

34

in a low voice, "Give it... her."

When Mrs Greenough had departed with many fervent thanks, Maggie had gone back to find Mum collapsed on the settee, near-fainting. She had had to run and fetch Mum's smelling-salts and mix her a dose of sal hepetica, which was always an ominous sign.

"Whatever's the matter, Mum?"

"Oh, it's my nerves. What with your Daddy and the Germans..."

But Daddy and the Germans had been bad for *weeks*...

❋

Maggie put her key into the lock with a sinking heart. Mum had said she mightn't go into work at the shop today, if she didn't feel any better.

Maggie called out down the hall. There was no answer.

She called louder. Still no answer.

And then she noticed Mum's coat and hat were gone from the hall-stand. So she had gone to work after all. She must be feeling better...

But hat and coat were no proof that Mum had gone to work really. She might be wandering round the town, still going mad...

Uneasily, Maggie sought the refuge of her bedroom. There were potatoes to peel, but they could wait. Mum might return too insane to cook them...

Maggie flung herself on to her bed and stared around her room, seeking comfort from old friends. The three teddies sat on their shelf as usual, leaning safely together; she never played with them now. Just put them under the bed for safety when the air-raid siren went.

There was her Dutch doll, fat and rosy-cheeked. Really, apart from the blackout curtain and the tape across the windows in big stars, her room looked no different from in peacetime, when Daddy had come home at five o'clock every night, and Mum had been always happy and singing.

How could some things change so, and yet other things stay the same?

Above her, the ceiling creaked. Her heart gave a terrified leap. And then she relaxed. She hadn't been frightened of the creaking ceiling for years, not since she was little and Daddy had explained it creaked because the sun made it hot and the beams expanded. Then night made it cool and the beams grew shorter again. And in growing longer or shorter, they made a creak.

She was getting as bad as Mum. She laughed, to try to make herself feel better.

Then the ceiling creaked again. And again. And a fourth time. It never did *that*. Not four times in a row, straight off. It was almost as if something heavy was moving about up there... some heavy creature...

And the next time it creaked, she swore she saw the ceiling *move*. And a little tiny speck of whitewash broke loose and twinkled down. Slowly. Like a tiny parachute...

And that set her thinking about the German parachutists, descending in their hundreds over the skies of Holland and Belgium, so the sky was black with them, in the cinema newsreels.

And they said they did not come as soldiers, but as spies, saboteurs. Disguised as nuns and clergymen, they had blown up bridges and ammunition dumps.

Billie Cramer said they were landing in England after dark already. Disguised as bus conductors and Salvation Army.

She lay frozen with fear, listening.

A sound came down through the ceiling. It sounded very like a groan... a soft groan.

She leapt off the bed, trembling from head to foot. There *was* somebody up there, in the loft. Was *that* why Mum was so terrified? But why had Mum run off and left her? Alone with it?

Oh, she told herself, this is silly. This is England! This is our house, 17 Bretton Gardens.

It was a charm she had often used; but this time it didn't work.

And then came a sound that brought just a tiny bit of comfort.

A snore? *Was* it a snore? She had to be sure.

Silently, gingerly, she put her bedside chair on to her chest of drawers and climbed up and listened, the slightly-damp pungent smell of the ceiling plaster and whitewash filling her nostrils.

She put her ear right against the plaster, and then she knew it *was* snoring.

A sleeping spy? Was it safe to run for a policeman? But first....

But first she must be sure who he was. Just raise the trapdoor and peep, while he was asleep... Even if he wakened (and he sounded very deeply asleep) she could jump down and pull away the ladder, and run like mad and be out of the house long before he could catch her.

But first she went and opened the front door wide, so she could run straight out into the sunshine. And the next-door neighbour, old Mr Finnis, was busy mowing his lawn, and looked up to give her his usual smile.

It gave her the courage to go back to the ladder, the trapdoor, the loft.

She stood at the top of the ladder and pushed gently upwards on the trapdoor. It opened silently, giving out the usual smell of dust and mouse-droppings, soot and damp paper.

As usual, it seemed pitch-dark at first. Then the dim grey patch that was the skylight at the far end swam up into view, outlining the stacks of Daddy's old magazines, the push-chair she had had when she was a baby, the old cabin-trunk and suitcases. All as usual.

But what was not usual was a pile of what seemed to be old coats and rugs. She was *sure* they hadn't been there before.

And then the tangled pile of coats moved, and a foot pushed out of the bottom. A very large foot with a grey sock on it, and a big hole in the end of the sock and a big toe sticking out of it.

For a long time, holding her breath 'til it hurt, she studied the toe.

A man's toe, a big man's toe, a sleeping man's toe.

But otherwise it told her nothing new. And she felt reluctant to report to her future policeman that she had only seen a toe. She felt her policeman would not be convinced by just a toe. She must know a little more. A German uniform, a nun's habit, or at least a *face*.

And the sight of the sock with the hole in it had made her a little bolder. It had made its owner seem a lot less frightening. Not a very *good* spy. Perhaps, even... a harmless old tramp. What a fool she would seem reporting a spy, if it was just a tramp!

If she came two more steps up the ladder she could slide her body along the floor from the trap-door, peer round the piles of Daddy's magazines and *see* the man's face.

One step up, two. Raise the trapdoor higher.

Silently, begin to slide her chest across the floorboards, through the dust that made her want to sneeze...

The huge hand descended on the collar of her school coat without warning; dragged her in, the whole length of her, like she was a mewling puppy. Behind her, she heard the trap-door bang shut.

The rancid smell of a filthy male animal filled her nostrils. A great filthy face loomed up at her through the darkness...

"Maggie!" said a voice.

And she was in Daddy's arms.

*

"We didn't want you to know," he said wretchedly, when the cuddling had finally stopped. "It was just to be a secret between Mummy and me."

"But why. You're *safe!* Is Martha all right?"

"Poor Martha went for a burton outside Amiens. She was caught in a mass of refugees. They blocked the road so we couldn't get through. Then a Stuka put a bomb into her. She burnt for hours. I kept looking back and seeing smoke."

She felt Daddy shudder and knew there was more he was not telling her.

"How did you escape?"

"Hiding in ditches. Four days, hiding in ditches."

"But you don't need to hide now!"

He said, in a low voice, "They left us, Maggie. The officers left us and ran away. In a staff car. They left us to get killed. They didn't care – only about saving their own skins. And we got bombed and machine-gunned.

"I'm not going back to that. The army's finished. We had to leave all our tanks and guns and lorries over there, for the Jerries to get. We've got nothing left to fight with."

"You're not…"

"Yes I am. I'm a deserter. I've run away too."

It was beyond belief. Bad beyond belief. Her daddy. A deserter.

She closed her eyes. What would the kids at school say, when they knew?

What would Billie Cramer say? What would the headmaster say?

Life would be an endless misery… she shrank away from him.

"I'll go away," he said, humbly. "I'll go away and never bother you and Mum again."

Oh, she had loved him so much and now she hated him so much. She turned to him and said, "Who's going to look after England? Who's going to look after *us?*"

"Would you rather have me *dead?*"

His dirty face appealed to her; there was sweat on his brow in the grey light of the skylight.

She got up stiffly and dusted her skirt.

"Yes," she said with hate, and turned and walked to the trap-door, opened it, let herself down on to the ladder and out of the house.

*

The police picked her up at near midnight, walking, still walking on the promenade. When they took her home, her mum was frantic. Asked her where she'd been, what she'd been doing?

But somehow she knew it was all pretend. Mum knew very well what she'd been doing, because Dad must have told her.

Before he went.

Back to the Army.

Never to have to fight again. Never to have to leave England, through all the long years of war. Which he spent at an ordnance depot in the north of Scotland, running lorry-loads of spares to ack-ack gun sites that never fired in anger.

And, after the war, that evening after school was never mentioned.

She almost came to believe it might have been a dream.

OPERATION
CROMWELL

The summer of 1940 was a bad time for us. My father was a dairy farmer. Before the war he was also a butter-factor.

He bought butter off the other farmers, and blended nineteen different sorts together to make the perfect butter that graced the tables of the grand hotels on the sea front at Bournemouth and Eastbourne. It took days, and knowledge; he was a real craftsman.

But when the war came the government stopped all that. We had to sell all our butter to them, so they could cut it up in tiny portions to sell on the rations.

All the profit would've been gone; my father always got an extra twopence a pound for his special butter. And those hotels were fuller than ever, with all sorts of high-ranking officers dining out their own wives, or others.

Where would the running of the war

have been if those high-ranking officers didn't have their proper food?

So we only sold so much of our butter to the government; the rest still went to the hotels. The newspapers might call us Black Marketeers, but I reckon we were a vital part of the war effort.

We moved our special butter around after dark, secretly, in my dad's old car. The car was special, in so far as it had a little boot most other cars didn't have, under the back seat. You could only get to it by lifting the seat up on the inside.

It worked a treat, 'til the summer of 1940 and the fall of France. Then Anthony Eden, the Foreign Secretary, came on the radio, and called for fit men between sixteen and sixty to volunteer for the Home Guard. On the news they said that a million men had come forward in the first week.

A million nuisances! Us lads went to watch our local Home Guard drilling in our schoolyard. We were a bit mad, because we'd used to play football in that yard in the evenings.

To us it was *our* yard. But they just nicked it, without a by-your-leave. And what a mess they were! A lot of those useless individuals didn't know their right foot from their left.

They were drilled by the landlord of the pub, who'd been a sergeant in the Royal Engineers. He had a bellow like a bull; we soon learnt to imitate it to perfection, and we'd stand there shouting "About turn!" in his voice, and having them marching slap into the entrance of the girls' toilets. Laugh!

Finally, he'd get so mad he'd come tearing out of the gate and chase us. But he never caught anybody but little Billy Swan, who'd only come to watch and who wasn't shouting false drill-commands at all. I mean, if they couldn't catch kids, how were they going to catch Jerry paratroopers?

But they were soon on patrol, defending Britain's shores by night because they were too busy making a living during the day.

I'm glad the Germans didn't come then. Those Home Guard were a sight! They only had half the uniforms they needed, but they'd shared them out so that some had battledress tops over their usual corduroy trousers, and others had battledress trousers with a clean white shirt on top, that their wives had carefully ironed for them. So the Jerries could see them clearly in the dark, I suppose!

They had three shotguns among them and the rest had hayforks. And they had this little Austin Ten which the blacksmith had turned into an armoured car with sheets of half-inch steel, which made it so heavy that the tyres ran nearly flat and it could only do about five miles an hour.

But they still used it for the only thing they were good for. Road-blocks. They'd pick any road at random and half-block it with their armoured car, and stop every car that passed and search it for Nazi spies and saboteurs, and secret radios and explosives and such.

It didn't help our butter-smuggling at all. My father did what he could. He joined the Home Guard himself, with the idea that the Home Guard wouldn't stop and search a mate's car, especially if the mate was in Home Guard uniform.

And my father had a full Home Guard uniform straight away, cap and all, because he slipped a couple of pounds of butter to the Home Guard quartermaster at Brighton.

Because, you might say, butter greased us a smooth path through the war. Fish fresh off the fishing boats, bacon off the pig farmers – you could get anything with a little bit of butter. Even the fags the tobacconists kept under the counter for their special customers.

But Dad's uniform didn't help all that much because we had to pass outside our own Home Guard area on the way to Bournemouth or Eastbourne. And those blokes were fanatics.

They'd even search the Vicar's car! They'd even bring their *wives* to strip-search *nuns*, because everyone said that the Nazi paratroopers who dropped in Holland and France and Belgium had been disguised as vicars and nuns. The Church had a very hard time of it.

My dad's next idea was to ensconce my Auntie Maude in the back seat of his car. She weighed thirteen stone, and in her fur coat she just filled the whole back seat. And she said she had such bad rheumatics in her knees that it took four strong men to lever her out once she was in.

Since no one in their right mind could mistake her for a paratrooper (they never made parachutes that big!) the Home Guard usually gave up while she was still stuck halfway out through the door. (Mind you, she could get out nippily enough once we took her home afterwards, with her little pound of butter.)

Anyway, with me in the front passenger seat and Auntie Maude in the back, we got clean away with it. Until the fatal night of September 7th, 1940.

We were halfway to Dover that night, on the lonely road across the downs, when Auntie Maude suddenly yelled, "Stop!" We screeched to a halt. (Auntie Maude in the back was very hard on the breaks.)

"What?" roared my father, looking around furtively at the totally empty dark road.

"I thought I heard church bell ringing," said Auntie Maude.

We all listened with bated breath then. Because the ringing of the church bells had been forbidden, except in the case of the Invasion. They were meant to be *the* warning of the Invasion.

But all we heard was the night breeze.

My father let out an explosive sigh of relief.

"They're only ringin' inside her head," he muttered. "She's suffered from tinnitus since she was a girl."

To her he said, "The Nazis won't get you tonight, Maude."

"It's not that I'm worried about," she

snapped. "It's me butter."

My father let off the handbrake and drove on. But after about a mile, he braked again, with a curse. Beyond the dim glow of our blacked-out headlights, something bigger than any man was moving in the road.

I peered ahead nervously, trying to make it out. Wondering about Frankenstein's Monster and Nazi secret weapons...

"It's a horse," said my father, in disbelief. "A horse with a girl on its back."

He wound down the window and shouted, "Can I help you?" in a pretty rude voice. He hasn't much time for the local hunt; he reckons they break his hedges and frighten the cows, and cut down the milk yield.

"Oh, I say," called the girl, in a voice that did remind me of our local hunt, "You haven't seen any Nazi paratroopers, have you?"

"Now why should you ask a daft question like that?" asked my father heavily.

The girl had come closer; the horse was very excited and restive with foam round its mouth, and I think Dad was scared it might damage the car. It was a very large horse.

"Haven't you heard?" asked the girl, dismounting. Her eyes were like saucers. "The code-word's gone out. Cromwell. To the army and the Home Guard. It means the Invasion has started."

"Oh aye?" said my father, very disbelieving. "Where?"

"I was in Dover," said the girl. "And at nine o'clock tonight all the trumpets sounded from the Castle Cliff."

"Perhaps they're having a band practice?" said my father.

"No, it *is* the Invasion. The Germans have dug a secret tunnel across the Channel and are coming on the surface near Lympne. My job is to cover the Downs and report any paratroopers by public telephone. I've got my money ready, you see!" She held up two big round pennies.

"Well, the Best of British Luck, miss," said Dad, and put the car into gear again.

"Women!" he said savagely, half a mile down the road.

"I thought I heard those church bells," said Auntie Maude.

"*Damn* women!" said my father, even more savagely.

We were stopped at the next village by a bunch of men in sports jackets carrying halberds; that strange mixture of spear and axe.

My father gave a growl and would have driven straight through them, I swear, except they'd blocked the road with two farm carts.

Instead he screeched, "Are you the Home Guard?"

I mean, we knew the Home Guard was feeble, but...

"Not exactly," said a beautiful, well-modulated voice. "We're actually a touring company of *The Yeomen of the Guard*, giving performances to the troops to raise morale. Working out of Drury Lane... but we thought we'd better do our bit."

"Your bit of what?"

"Haven't you heard the church bells? The Invasion's on. The Germans have got a secret tunnel under the Channel and they're firing torpedoes at Dover Harbour from it... and they've captured the RAF airfield at Lympne and are flying their planes off it already."

My father looked very pointedly at the tranquil night sky, lit only by the pink glow that hung over burning London.

"Where are the planes then?"

"Well, of course, I say, they couldn't fly at night. But ..."

"Please let me past," said my father coolly.

"I am in the real Home Guard. Engaged on a mission of Vital National Importance."

"Ooh I say, Gerald, better let the blighter past, what?"

There was a deep consultation and they finally pulled back the farm carts, then stood back waving and shouting, "The Best of British Luck!"

We should have turned back then, but my father's a stubborn cuss.

Two miles further on we were flagged down by two real policemen.

"Can I be of assistance, officer?" asked my dad with a kind of nervous authority, as my heart sank.

"I am requisitioning this car, sir, under the Emergency Powers Act. The Invasion has started. They're coming ashore up the beach at Brighton. Please drive us to Dover Police Station, immediately."

Well, there was no arguing with that. One huge policeman squeezed in alongside Auntie Maude, and the other sat in the front with me on his knee. What with all that load of butter, the poor little car sounded like it was on its last legs. It was lucky it was downhill nearly all the way.

But at a road junction, about five miles

out of Dover, we heard a sound that even dwarfed the labouring wheezing of our engine. A hideous squealing of metal; a screeching, a squeaking like all the devils in hell were loose in rusty armour.

"Wossat?" gasped Dad, cutting the engine and cowering down in his seat.

"Tanks," said the policeman in front. "I've heard it before. There's no other sound like it."

"Reckon it's Jerry?" asked the other policeman in a whisper. "Them Panzers move fast – blitzkrieg they call it, lightning war. Reckon they could ha' made it this far from Brighton?"

"I'm not taking no chances," said the other. "Into the hedge, quick! Them Panzers'll shoot on sight."

We all dived into the hedge. I've never seen Auntie Maude move so fast in her life.

The screeching had grown unbearable by the time the first tank came round the bend.

It was huge. It filled the whole width of the road. There were sparks flying from its tracks... It passed without stopping, though the commander on top looked hard at our poor little car.

"S'aright," muttered one policeman.

"They're British. Matildas. Them's the ones that shot Jerry to bits outside Dunkirk. Made Dunkirk possible. If only we'd had more of them."

I wanted to jump up and cheer, they looked so big and grand and powerful. But the policeman pressed me flat.

"Stay still, son. The British'll be firing at anything that moves an' all. They'll be trigger-happy tonight."

There were only four tanks, in the end.

"Not enough," said one policeman sadly.

"Hope they're not retreating already," said the other.

They were trying to sound brave for our benefit. But I could feel the one next to me shivering and he smelt funny. It was then I really began to believe the Invasion was happening.

We reached the police station eventually. The forecourt was absolute chaos – police, army, even Navy trucks. Everyone running around yelling their heads off. I suppose we should have been scared of being caught as Black Marketeers by the police, but it was just lost in fear of the Germans.

An officer in a tin hat ran up.

"I'm commandeering this car," he

shouted. "I must get ammunition up to D Company and our truck's broken down. It's urgent. The men have only got five rounds apiece for their rifles and they're guarding Shakespeare Cliff. Out, out, out."

We got out shivering, and six men ran up carrying flat heavy wooden boxes, one between two. Boxes about as big as our box of butter.

"There's not room for it all inside, sir," panted a man.

"Yes there is," snapped the officer. "My father's got a car like this. There's a boot hidden under the back seat. Get the seat up."

Up came the back seat. Out came our box of butter on to the forecourt of the police station.

"What you got in here?" shouted one soldier. "Lead?"

"Personal possessions," said my father hastily, looking round. But our two policemen had been lost in the chaos.

"What shall we do?" wailed Auntie Maude, looking very hard at the butter box.

"Sit on it," snapped my father. He was always a quick-thinking man.

The box vanished utterly under the skirts of Auntie Maude's fur coat.

"Right, sir," said the officer to my father. "Will you drive us up to Shakespeare Cliff? "I'll show you the way."

We spent the rest of the night driving, defending Britain. We saw a lot of soldiers, guns, tanks, policemen and refugees starting to panic and take to the roads.

What we never saw was Germans. Not a trace. And as the night went on, the place they were landing seemed to get further and further away. Eastbourne, Bournemouth, Portland Bill, Lyme Regis in Dorset, Exmouth, Plymouth...

✳

We were actually pulling in to area HQ with a request for hand-grenades when we saw an officer with red on his cap standing stretching his arms on the tarmac in the pink dawn and, from the very way he stretched, I just knew the Germans had never come.

"Load of stuff and nonsense, old boy. All the code-name 'Cromwell' was meant to mean was 'Invasion Imminent'. But it never happened."

"Right, thanks chaps," said our officer to us. "Stand down. Duty well done. Sorry I can't invite you to breakfast in the mess."

The world was beautiful; England was still free; the cool morning air seemed like champagne, the best we'd ever breathed.

All we had to worry about was getting our Black Market butter from the police station.

Funny how one terror can replace another. People went to prison for Black Marketeering. Our local mayor was serving three months for a fuss about a side of bacon. It was like walking into the lion's den...

But, glory be, in the clear morning light, after a night of cold and terror, Auntie Maude was still dutifully sitting there on the forecourt. And a nice young constable was just giving her an enamel mug of tea.

Why did she have to stand up when she saw us? Stand up and wave?

"Hell*ooh*," said the nice young constable. "What's all this?"

He reached down and opened the lid of the box. Stared at all the serried rows of packets of butter.

"Butter," he said to himself. And gave Auntie Maude a very hard look.

It was then that Auntie Maude excelled herself.

"I dunno," she wrinkled up her face. "It was just somewhere to sit. My legs were hurting. Some fellers left it there. They had Welsh accents. Asked me to keep an eye on it for them."

"What did they look like?" He was still suspicious.

"I don't know, ducky. It was dark, wasn't it?"

"Hey, Sarge!" called the constable...

"Inspector, sir?" called the sergeant...

Even the Superintendent came out.

"Must be Black Market stuff," said my dad, helpfully.

All the coppers looked at him.

"What are you doing here?" the Superintendent asked.

"Me and my car got commandeered by the Army. I had to leave our Maude with you for safety."

"Right," said the Superintendent. "Well, we'll take this butter in charge, thank you very much. Good day to you!"

His expression had turned from suspicion to gratification. You could tell he was thinking about breakfast...

He walked away, with two constables carrying it behind. But I saw them lifting the lid and helping themselves to half-pound packs and shoving them into their pockets before they even got through the police station door.

Ten quid's worth of our best butter. That would have paid a farm labourer's wages for a month.

As I said, 1940 was a bad time for us.

ROSIE

Rosie cut down Lime Street, walking fast. Not easy in the blackout. But there was a moon tonight, flirting with the clouds. A bomber's moon.

Rosie was an ARP warden; air-raid patrol, a full-timer and proud of it. She liked being one of the few women wardens, even if she'd had to lie about her age to get in. She was only eighteen, but big with it.

She liked the comradeship of the Warden's Post. She liked all the new people she met.

Before the War she'd been a mother's help. A comfy life, but not a lot of thrills. Changing nappies; wheeling prams round Seffie Park. She'd loved the babies and they had loved her, but it hadn't been getting her anywhere.

Now she was meeting new people from morning 'til night. And she usually called in at some dance, after she came off duty.

Strange, dancing in her warden's uniform; but there were plenty of girls in uniform now, Wrens and Waafs.

She met such interesting fellers. Tonight's bloke had lived in Australia and caught crocodiles with his bare hands to sell to zoos. Last week she'd met a cheerful undertaker, serving with the Irish Guards. The way he'd eyed her, she hadn't been sure he wasn't measuring her up for a coffin!

She liked a good time; but she wasn't a good-time girl. She always went home before eleven. Alone. That way, fellers didn't get the wrong idea.

Liverpool was safe enough. Nothing worse than some amorous drunk you had to hold up while he was talking to you. Easy enough to get away from *them*; they usually fell over when you let go of them.

The worst thing that could happen was you might fall into one of those great gaping pigswill bins in the dark, stinking of potato peelings and boiled-out fish-heads.

It was lonely, out on the streets. Her sharp footsteps echoed off the tall buildings, but her gas mask case and tin hat banged against her bottom reassuringly.

And the pubs might be dark, but they

were full to bursting behind their blackout curtains; roared-out choruses of *We'll Meet Again* and *Roll Out The Barrel* cheered her on her way.

Mind you, the war was terrible for some people; like those poor people down that shelter in Mellor Street. The bomb had burst outside the door and killed them all with the blast. With hardly a mark on them, even the little kids.

But Mellor Street wasn't in Rosie's district and you only worried about your own district now. Rosie's district had had a few bombs, a few people buried under the rubble. But she'd helped to dig them out with her bare hands, working shoulder to shoulder with the fellers; and held their hands till the ambulance came. She'd cheered them up and that made her feel good.

Rosie hurried on. The pubs were further apart now and even the alleys were silent. Just the odd moggie, poor things, scavenging at the pigswill bins.

She was just bending down to stroke one when the siren went. For the third time that day. Rosie got the usual sinking feeling in her gut, but she wasn't all that worried. Air-raid sirens couldn't kill you. She listened intently, through the dying drone of the siren, for the sound of bombers' engines...

And heard nothing.

She'd carry on for a bit, try and get home before anything happened. Her ma would worry if she was caught out in a raid. Ma might even leave the shelter and come looking for her, as far as the chippie in Scobie Street. Then batter Rosie over the ear when she found her, for causing so much worry.

"G'night, moggie. Best of British Luck!"

Her footsteps quickened; the gas mask banged harder against her bottom, as if urging her on.

She'd gone nearly half a mile before she heard the bombers coming. She was in a district she hardly knew. Really poor people, to judge from the state of their doors and windows. But you couldn't be choosy when the bombers came. You just ran for the nearest brick street-shelter with its concrete-slab roof.

Not many shelters round here. Poor people were always the worst looked after. Bet the toffs had shelters, and to spare, up Croxteth way...

She ran and ran. Turned a corner by a

chapel with bombed-out windows. Saw the three brass balls of a pawnbroker's... Then a great square shelter loomed up.

She made the doorway, just as the first guns opened up overhead, turning the night white-black, white-black. Making a noise like some daft kid banging a tin tray right in your ear that echoed across the whole sky after.

Then she heard the shrapnel shrieking down like dead rockets on Bonfire Night. And ducked through the blackout curtain into the shelter.

There was room by the door, on the slatted benches. She flung herself into it, to get her breath back. She must cut down on the ciggies; except it was hard to refuse when the men wardens offered them, friendly-like.

Still panting, she looked around.

And sighed. It seemed a totally miserable sort of shelter.

People huddled together in a dim blue light. Silent except for the racking cough and the dismal wail of a baby at the far end.

Some shelters were really jolly. Fellers brought a fiddle or a squeeze-box, and you could have a good sing-song to drown the

noise of the bombs. In some of the bigger ones there was dancing – a good knees-up as those Cockneys called it. In some there was even a drop to drink, or people passing round home-made toffee and biscuits.

Some even had buskers, doing their spoon-bashing or playing the *Air on a G String* on a musical saw. Or telling rude jokes that made the mums scream with laughter, and then tell their kids to put their hands over their ears so they couldn't hear.

But this was a bunch of real miserable sods. Looked really sorry for themselves. Nothing but cough, cough, wheeze and snore.

Might as well be dead, Rosie thought. Where there's life there's hope...

She caught the eye of an old feller opposite. She said, just to say something, "Big raid tonight. I expect they're copping it down the Dingle. Hope they don't hit the off-licence!"

The old man nodded, friendly enough; but he didn't say anything. Then he pursed his lips and shook his head, as if he was afraid she might wake the kid he was nursing on his lap.

God, even the kids were spiritless. In the

shelter at home they were always yelling for a condensed-milk buttie, or punching each other and chasing round the whole shelter, and getting their ears battered all the way round. What was the matter with this lot? Had they left their sense of humour at the pawnbroker's up the road?

So she told the only really dirty joke she knew. If that didn't get them laughing, it would take a thousand-pound bomb to shift them...

Again, the old man raised a finger to his lips.

Rotten old killjoy. Like the deacons in chapel when she was a kid. Children should be seen and not heard. No giggling in the House of God.

Cripes, she thought, this isn't a chapel, it's only a shelter. There must be *somebody* lively, further down...

She turned her head and shouted, "Are we downhearted?"

In her home shelter, the yell of "No!" would have raised the concrete roof two feet in the air, and made the Liver Birds rock on their perches.

Here, nothing. Silence.

Cough, cough. Wheeze. Snore. They

might as well be dead.

Chin up, she thought. Grin and bear it. Never say die.

But she didn't actually say any of those things. A chill was working into her, even through her thick warden's greatcoat. She shivered. And shivered again.

This shelter's damp, she thought. They've all caught bronchitis. She studied them intently in the dim blue light. They did look sort of ill; wrinkled, poverty-battered faces, mouths hanging open to show ill-fitting false teeth.

Unemployment, she thought, scrimping and saving and spreading marge on bread then scraping it off again. Years and years when hardly anybody's boat ever came in. Poor Liverpool! Let the poor souls rest in peace...

She shivered again. Shut up, Rosie, they haven't all been as lucky as you. The babies you looked after might have been boring, but at least you got four square meals a day, and a hottie in a nice clean bed at night. Count your blessings. Don't despise those who are worse off...

And then it began to bother her.

Where *was* that blue light coming from?

Normally the light in a shelter was yellow. Candles burning. Kids showing off their torches, flicking them round the ceiling. Or the hurricane lamps that the ARP laid on.

But the light was always *yellow*.

You only got blue lights in hospitals and factories, where they had mains electricity.

And there was no electricity in shelters. It was forbidden in law, in case the shelter was hit by a bomb and the broken electric cable-ends fried everyone to death.

So where *was* the blue light coming from?

Rosie stared around her.

It seemed to be coming from the people themselves. From their clothes, hands, faces... all over them.

"Where's the blue light coming from?" she shouted at the old man, a sudden cold fear gripping her heart.

With a ghastly little smile he raised his cap to her. Under his cap, his domed bald head was broken. Cracked open like an egg. Stuff oozing out.

She was up and out and running before she knew her legs had moved. Running through streets as bright as day with searchlights, shells and bombs exploding. But still she ran. She would have run into the mouth of Hell itself to get away from that shelter...

＊

It was the singing that stopped her in the end.

"There'll be bluebirds over, the White Cliffs of Dover..."

Another shelter. An accordion playing. People bellowing their lungs out.

She staggered inside. Every face turned to look at her. Interested grinning faces.

"Ey, whacker," said the warden by the door. "Catch your breath. You look like you've seen a ghost."

When Rosie finally caught her breath, luxuriating in the *yellow* candle-light, the hot breath from the singing, the little kids tripping over her legs, she asked the warden, "Do you know a street near here, wi' a bombed-out chapel and a pawnbrokers?"

He flinched, as if at some quite unbearably horrible memory.

"You mean Mellor... Street?" he asked.